Dear Parents,

Welcome to the Scholastic Reader series. We have taken over 80 years of experience with teachers, parents, and children and put it into a program that is designed to match your child's interests and skills.

Level 1—Short sentences and stories made up of words kids can sound out using their phonics skills and words that are important to remember.

Level 2—Longer sentences and stories with words kids need to know and new "big" words that they will want to know.

Level 3—From sentences to paragraphs to longer stories, these books have large "chunks" of texts and are made up of a rich vocabulary.

Level 4—First chapter books with more words and fewer pictures.

It is important that children learn to read well enough to succeed in school and beyond. Here are ideas for reading this book with your child:

- Look at the book together. Encourage your child to read the title and make a prediction about the story.
- Read the book together. Encourage your child to sound out words when appropriate. When your child struggles, you can help by providing the word.
- Encourage your child to retell the story. This is a great way to check for comprehension.
- Have your child take the fluency test on the last page to check progress.

Scholastic Readers are designed to support your child's efforts to learn how to read at every age and every stage. Enjoy helping your child learn to read and love to read.

— **Francie Alexander**
    Chief Education Officer
    Scholastic Education

For Gabe,

artist, farmer, rodeo queen

—D.M.

Compilation copyright © 1998 by David McPhail.
A Bug, a Bear, and a Boy and the Bath; A Bug, a Bear, and a Boy Play Hide-and-Seek;
A Bug, a Bear, and a Boy at Home; A Bug, a Bear, and a Boy Plant a Garden
Copyright © 1997 by David McPhail.
Activities copyright © 2003 Scholastic Inc.

Library of Congress Cataloging-in-Publication Data is available.

ISBN 0-590-14904-0

15 14 13 12 11 10   08 09 10 11 12

Printed in the U.S.A.   23
First printing, August 1998

A Bug, a Bear, and a Boy

by David McPhail

Scholastic Reader — Level 1

Cartwheel ·B·O·O·K·S· ®

SCHOLASTIC INC.

New York   Toronto   London   Auckland   Sydney
Mexico City   New Delhi   Hong Kong   Buenos Aires

Chapter 1

This is a bug.
The bug is little.

This is a bear.
The bear is big.

This is a boy.
The boy is bigger than the bug
and smaller than the bear.

The bear eats from a bucket.

The boy eats from a bowl.
And the bug eats from
a bottle cap.

They all read
from the same book.

Chapter 2

There go a bug, a boy,
and a bear.

The bear digs the dirt.

The bug plants seeds.
The boy waters them.

The seeds grow into plants.
A rabbit comes and eats them.

The bear chases the rabbit
away—

but the rabbit comes back.

The bug and the bear
and the boy build a fence.

Now the plants can grow.
And the rabbit can only watch.

Chapter 3

A boy, a bug, and a bear
play hide-and-seek.

The bear is big.
The bug and
the boy always
find him.

The boy is smaller
than the bear.
Sometimes the bug and
the bear find the boy.

Sometimes they do not.

The bug is little.

The bear and boy do not
find the bug.

They take a nap instead.

Chapter 4

The boy sits in the bath.
He has a boat.

The bug sits on the boat.

The bear is too big
to sit on the boat.
The bear is too big
to sit in the bath.
He sits on the floor.

The bear blows the boat.

He makes waves, too.
The waves are too big.

The boat tips over.
The boy saves the bug.

The bear saves the boat.

Then they all blow bubbles.

Chapter 5

The bear sleeps on a rug
on the floor.

The boy sleeps in a bed.
The bug sleeps in a peanut shell.

Good night, bug.
Good night, boy.
Good night, bear.